Smiffy

AND THE BIRTHDAY SURPRISE

Arcturus Publishing Limited
26/27 Bickels Yard
151–153 Bermondsey Street
London SE1 3HA

Published in association with
foulsham
W. Foulsham & Co. Ltd,
The Publishing House, Bennetts Close, Cippenham,
Slough, Berkshire SL1 5AP, England

ISBN 0-572-03085-1

British Library Cataloguing-in-Publication Data: a catalogue record for this
book is available from the British Library

This edition printed in 2005

Author: Chris Smith
Illustrator: Jim Hansen
Editor: Rebecca Gerlings

Printed in China

Smiffy

AND THE BIRTHDAY SURPRISE

Chris Smith
Illustrations Jim Hansen

ARCTURUS

Smiffy's eyes sprang open. He stretched his furry arms and leapt out of bed.

Suddenly, an excited feeling rushed from the tips of his ears right down to his toes. It bubbled and fizzed and tingled.

At once, Smiffy remembered
why he was excited.

Today was Jack's birthday. And birthdays meant … birthday parties! There would be party food and games and, best of all, *birthday cake!*

But birthdays also meant … birthday presents. Now, what would Jack like?

Smiffy scratched his head.

He rubbed his chin.

And suddenly the perfect idea
popped into his head.

At three o'clock that afternoon,
Smiffy knocked on Jack's front door.

He had his party clothes on and his magic
backpack on his back. (Smiffy never went
anywhere without his magic backpack.)

"HAPPY BIRTHDAY!" shouted Smiffy.

"Come inside!" said Jack…

…"The party's just beginning!"

Jack's party was fabulous!

They played
musical statues.
(Smiffy wobbled.)

They pinned the
tail on the
donkey.
(Smiffy lost.)

They passed the parcel. (Smiffy won!)

Soon it was time for Jack to open his presents.

His friends gave him…

a football,

a windmill,

a painting set…

…and **Boing!!!**

a jack-in-the-box!

Oh dear.

The jack-in-the-box landed – *splat!* – right in the middle of Jack's birthday cake.

It was ruined!

"Don't worry!" said Smiffy. "I haven't given you my birthday present yet."

He looked at his magic backpack and a brightly coloured parcel started to appear…

Everyone gathered round to watch Jack unwrap Smiffy's present. What could it be?

"Wow!" said Jack.
He held a black-and-
white apron and
a bowl and a big,
wooden spoon.

"Now you can
bake another
birthday cake,"
said Smiffy. "And
I'll help!"

Jack and Smiffy mixed together butter
and sugar and eggs and flour to
make a brand new birthday cake.

The kitchen got very messy.
The cake mixture got very sticky…

…and so did the chefs!

But it tasted great!

And when it came out of the oven it smelt delicious!

Jack spread
bright blue
icing on top
of the cake.

Then Smiffy stuck one … two … three … four … five … six … seven candles into the icing.

Perfect!

"Happy Birthday, Jack!" everyone shouted.
Jack blew the candles out
with one big puff.

"Make a wish, Jack,"
Smiffy said.

So Jack made a
secret wish.

Smiffy decided to make a wish, too.

He wished that every birthday party could

be as extra-special as this one.